How to Draw
ANIMALS

How to Draw
ANIMALS

Includes 60 Step-by-Step Instructions for Dogs, Cats, Birds, and More!

Racehorse Publishing

Racehorse Publishing books may be purchased in bulk at special discounts for sales promotion, corporate gifts, fund-raising, or educational purposes. Special editions can also be created to specifications. For details, contact the Special Sales Department, Skyhorse Publishing, 307 West 36th Street, 11th Floor, New York, NY 10018 or info@skyhorsepublishing.com.

Racehorse Publishing™ is a pending trademark of Skyhorse Publishing, Inc.®, a Delaware corporation.

Visit our website at www.skyhorsepublishing.com.

10 9 8 7 6 5 4 3 2 1

Cover and interior artwork: Diego Jourdan Pereira

ISBN: 978-1-63158-706-1

Printed in China

Previously published as two separate volumes:
Learn to Draw Animals (ISBN: 978-1-63158-239-4)
and *Learn to Draw Pets* (ISBN: 978-1-944686-24-6).

How to Draw
ANIMALS

1

2

3

4

5

Practice Page

Practice Page

1

2

3

4

5

Practice Page

Practice Page

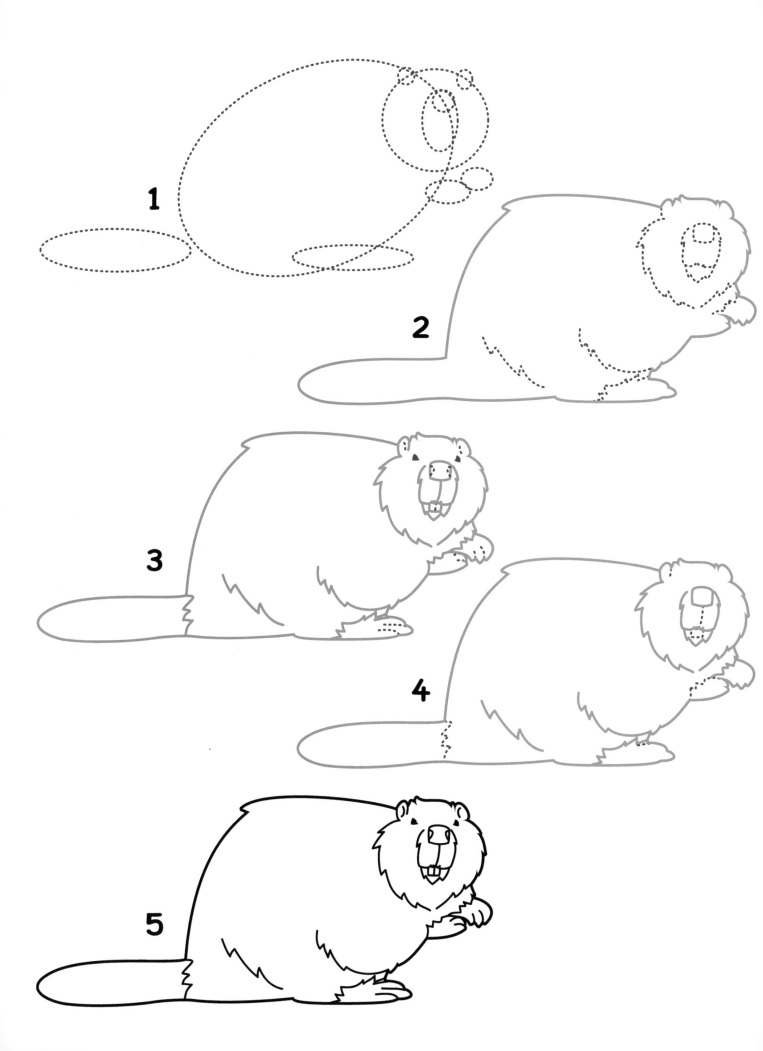

1

2

3

4

5

Practice Page

Practice Page

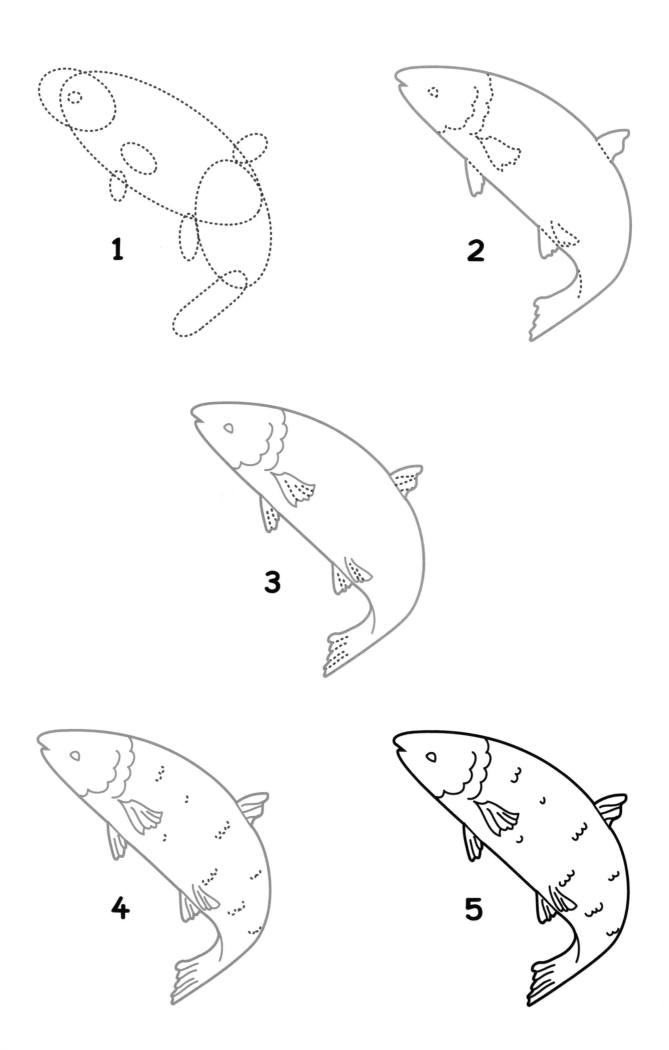

Practice Page

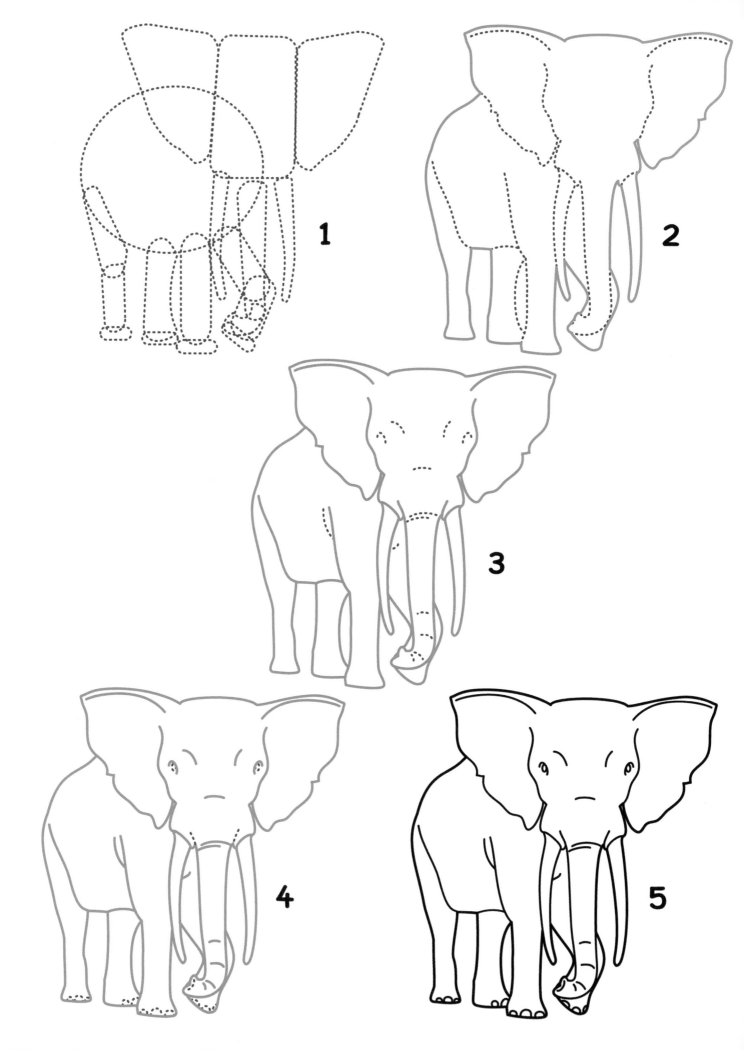

Practice Page

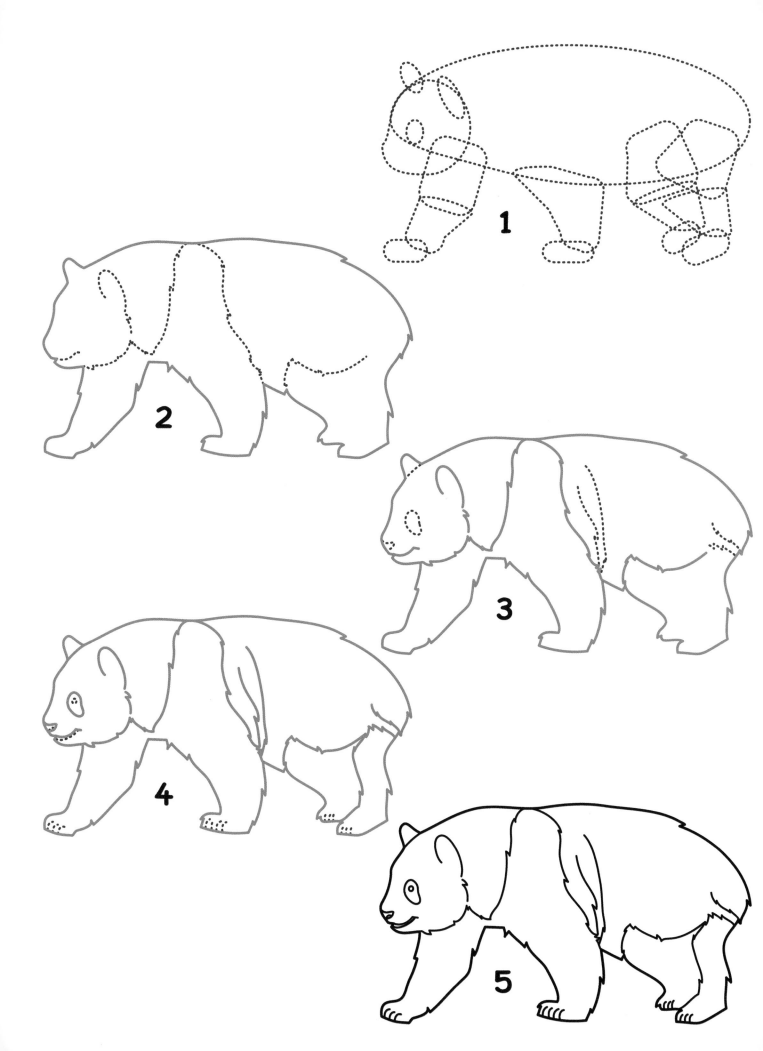

Practice Page

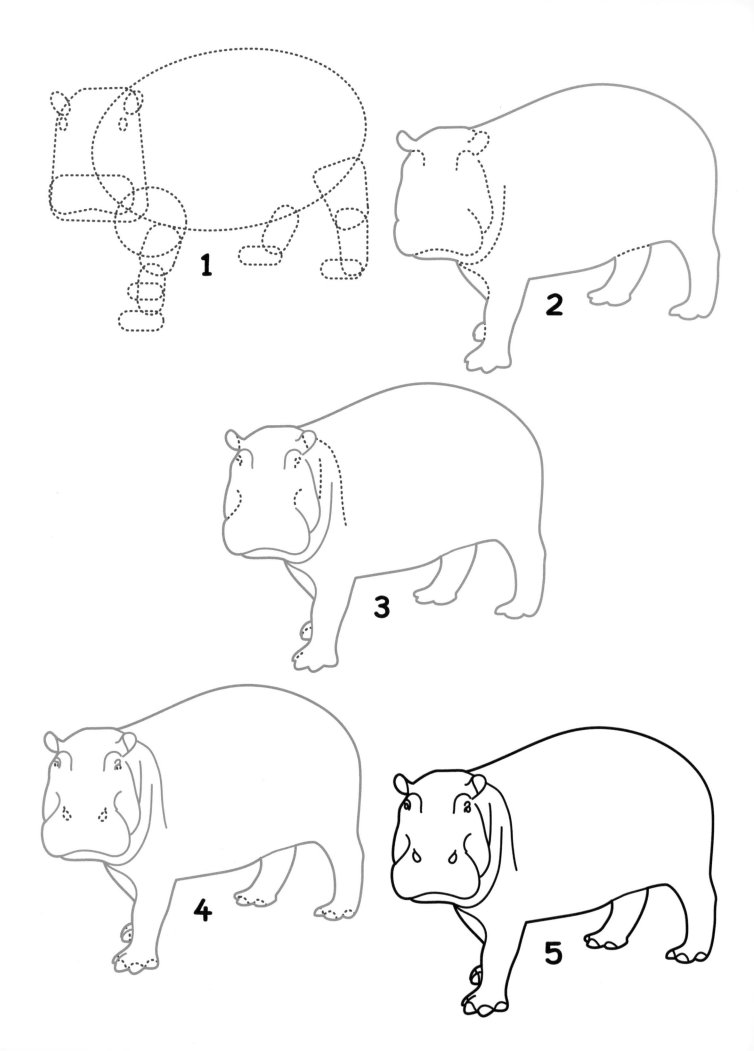

Practice Page

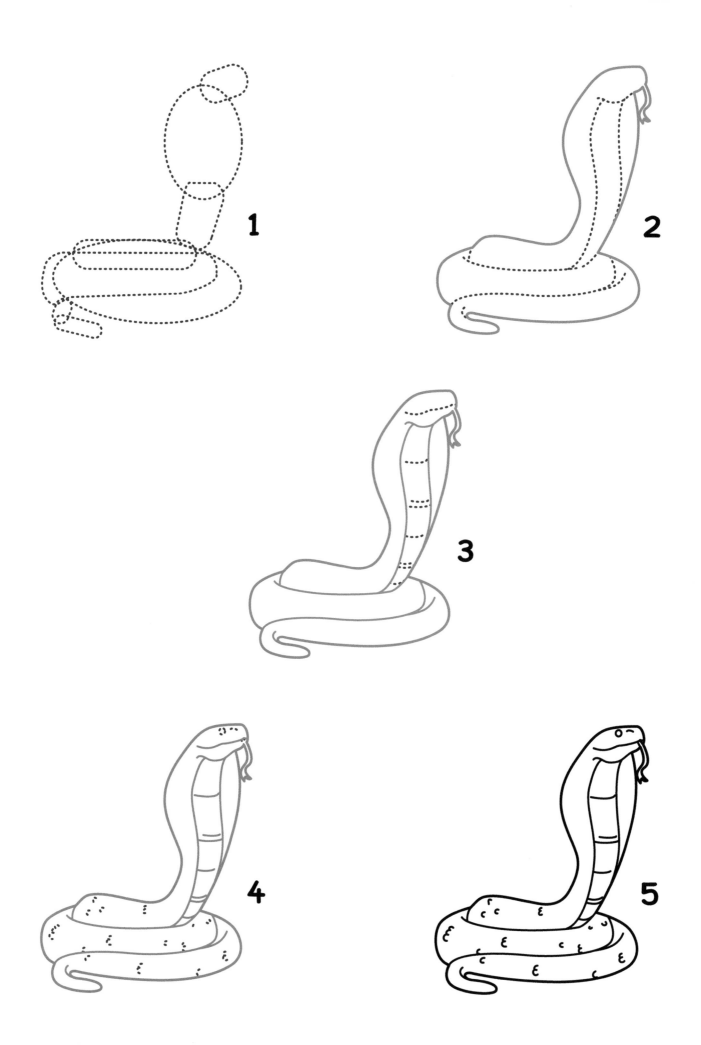

Practice Page

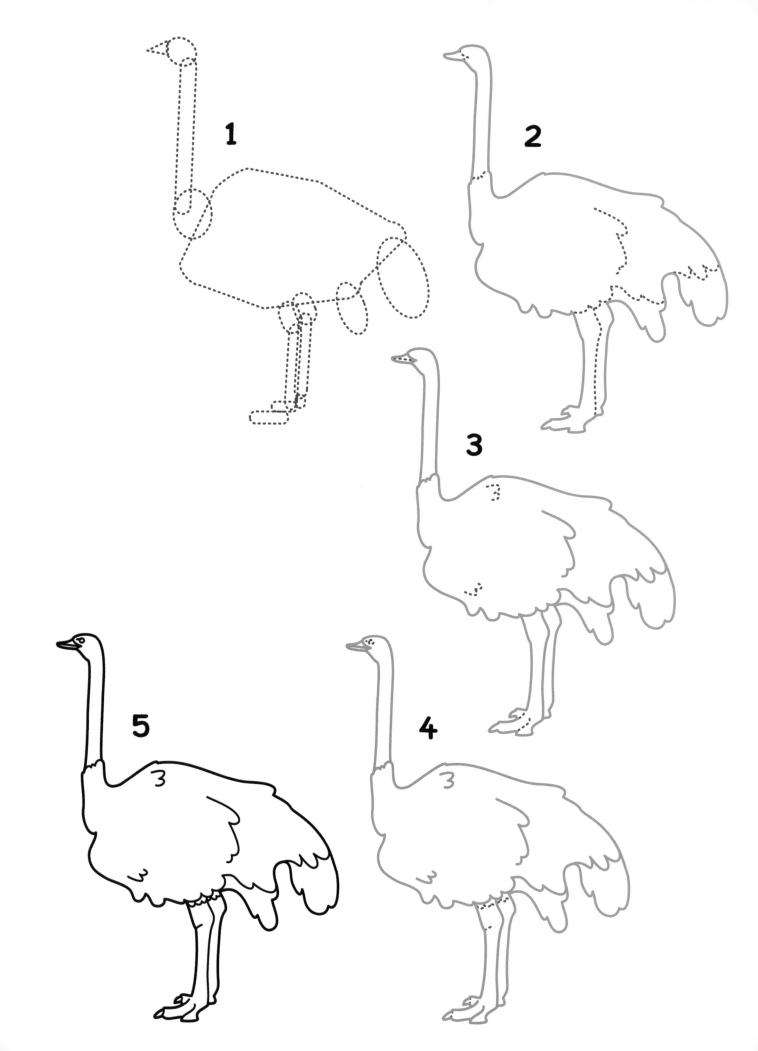

Practice Page

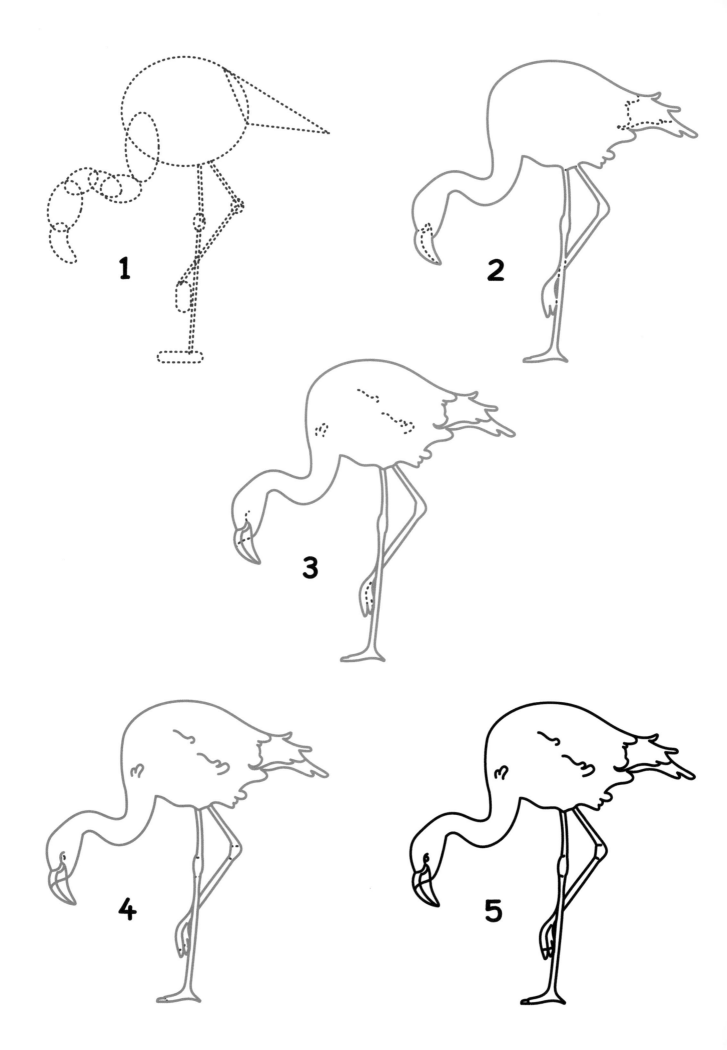

Practice Page

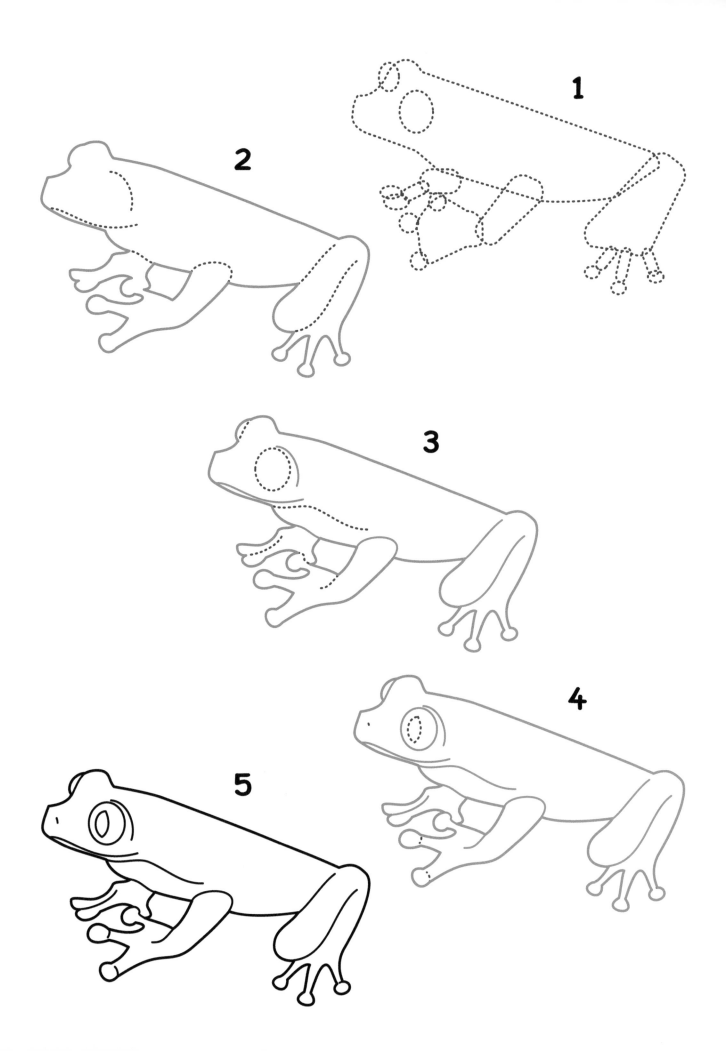

Practice Page

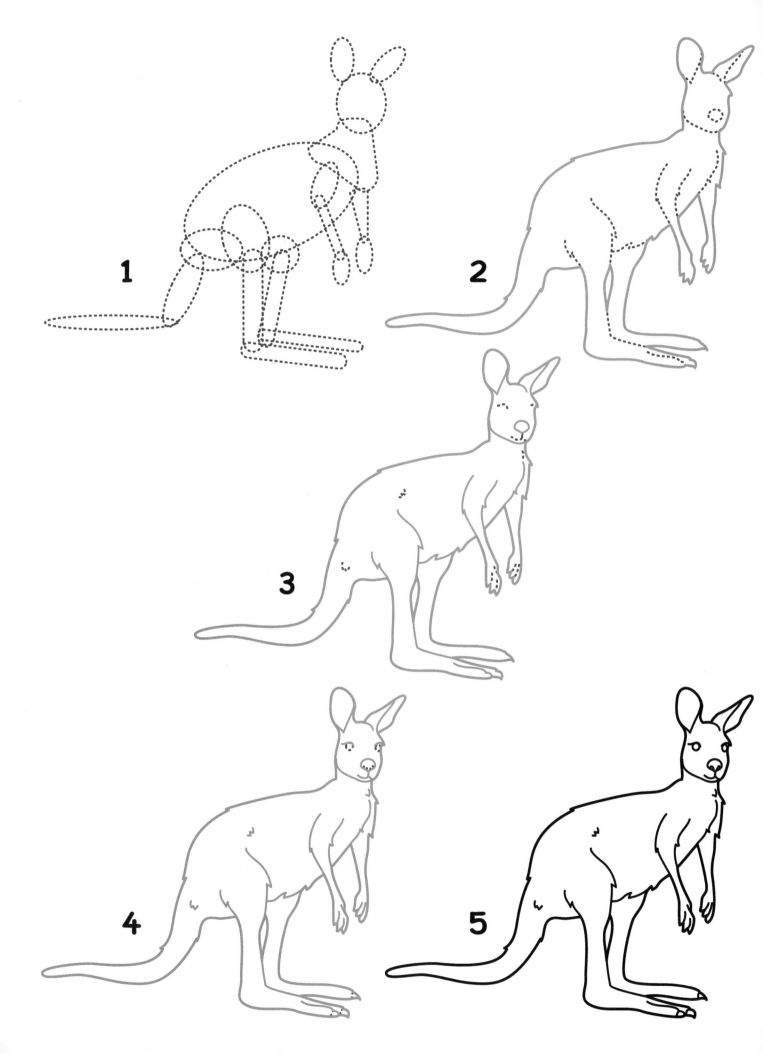

1

2

3

4

5

Practice Page

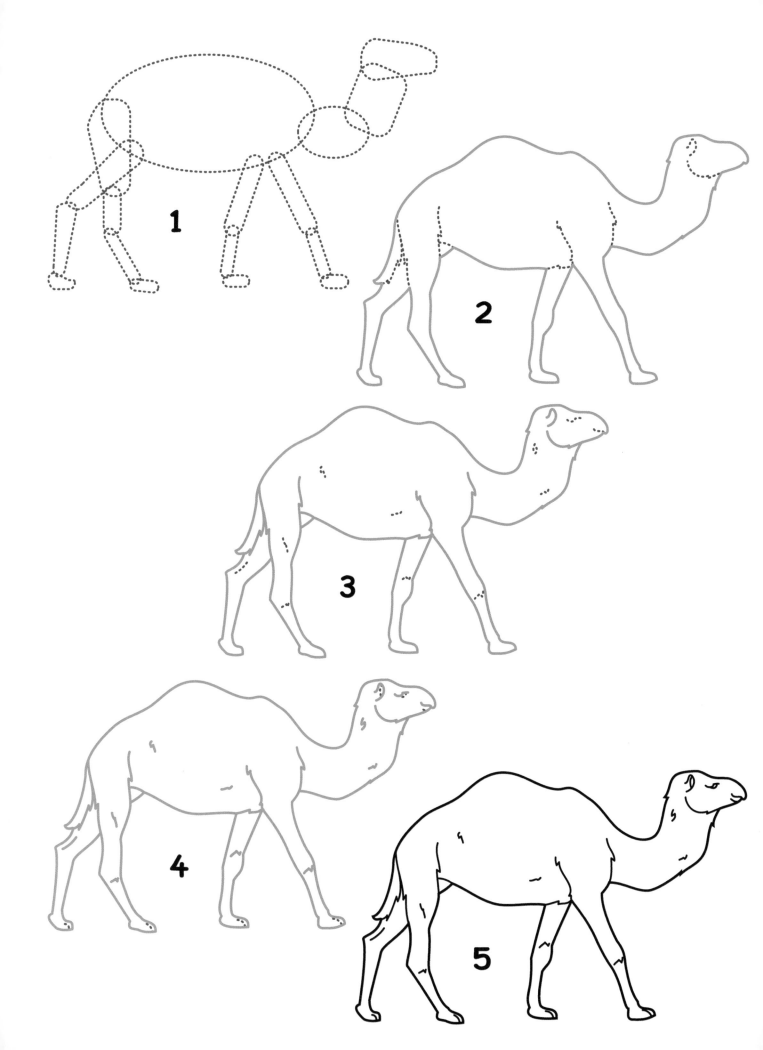

Practice Page

Practice Page

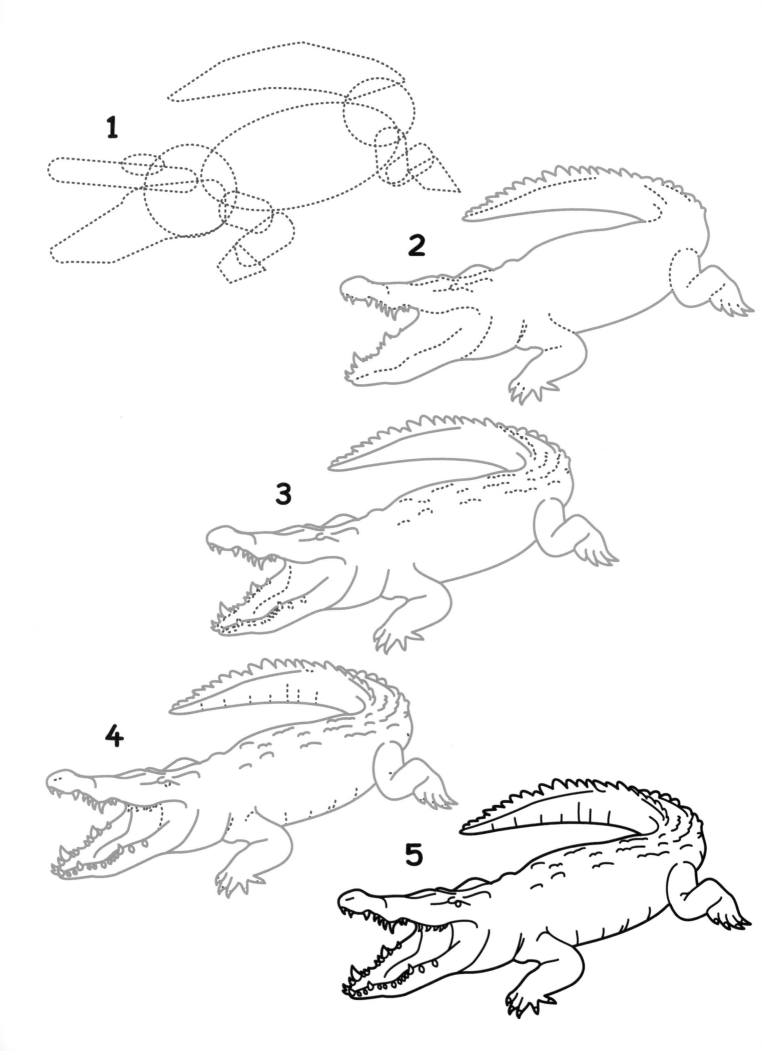

Practice Page

Practice Page

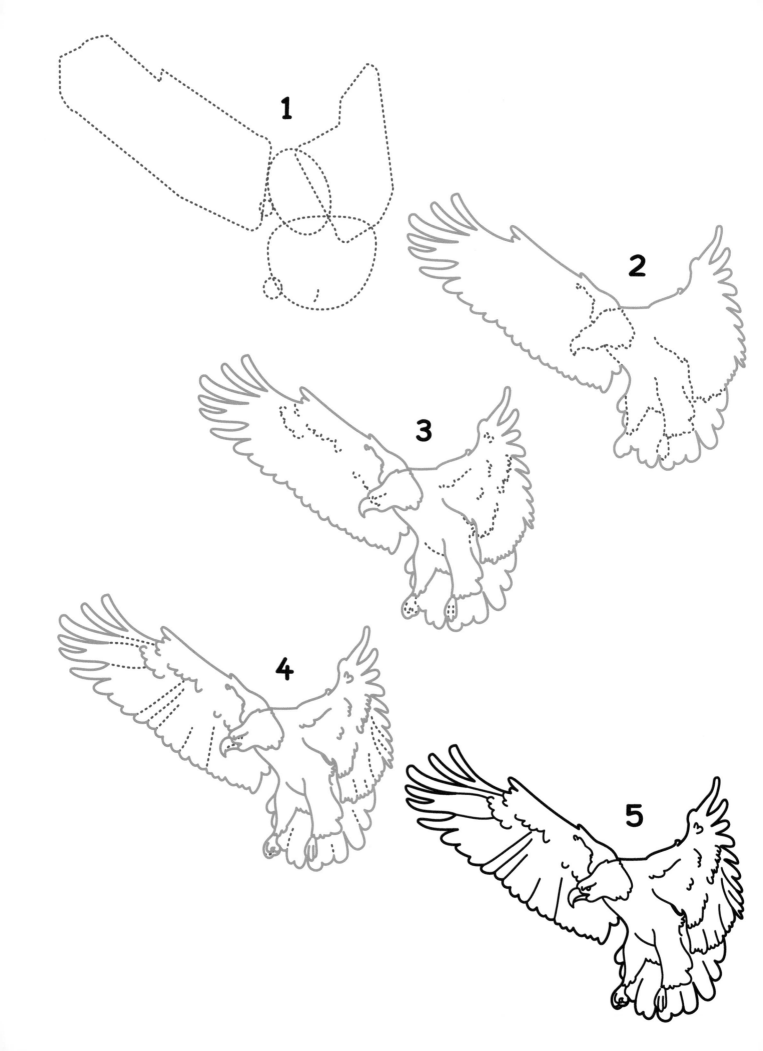

Practice Page

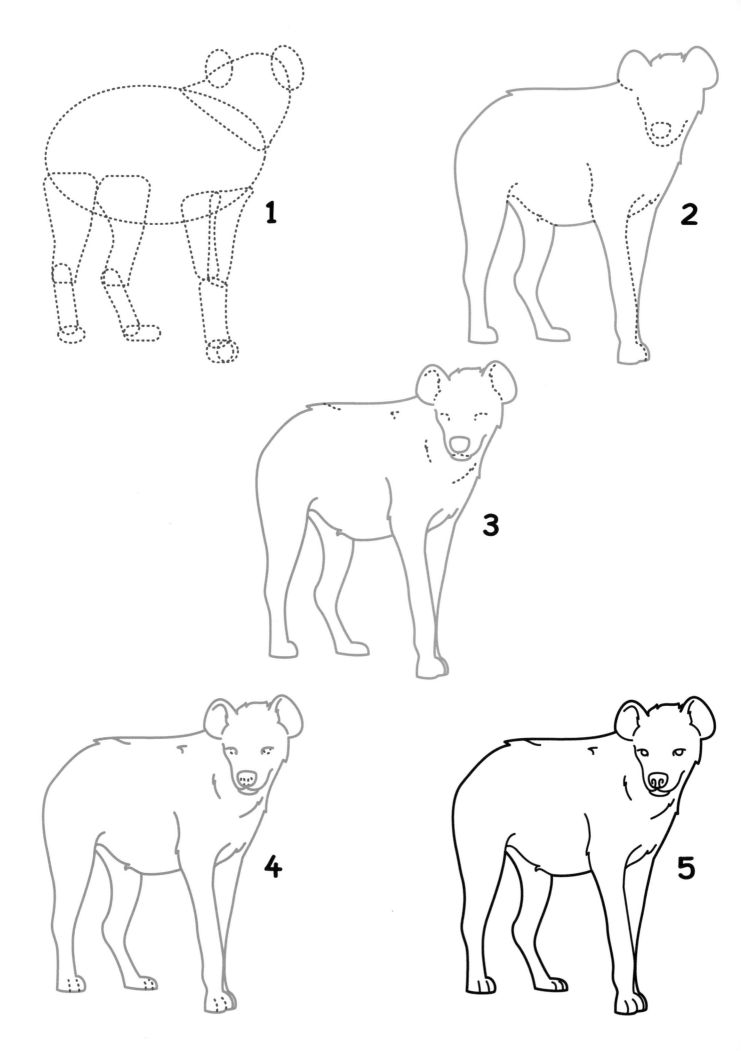

Practice Page

Practice Page

1

2

3

4

5

Practice Page

Practice Page

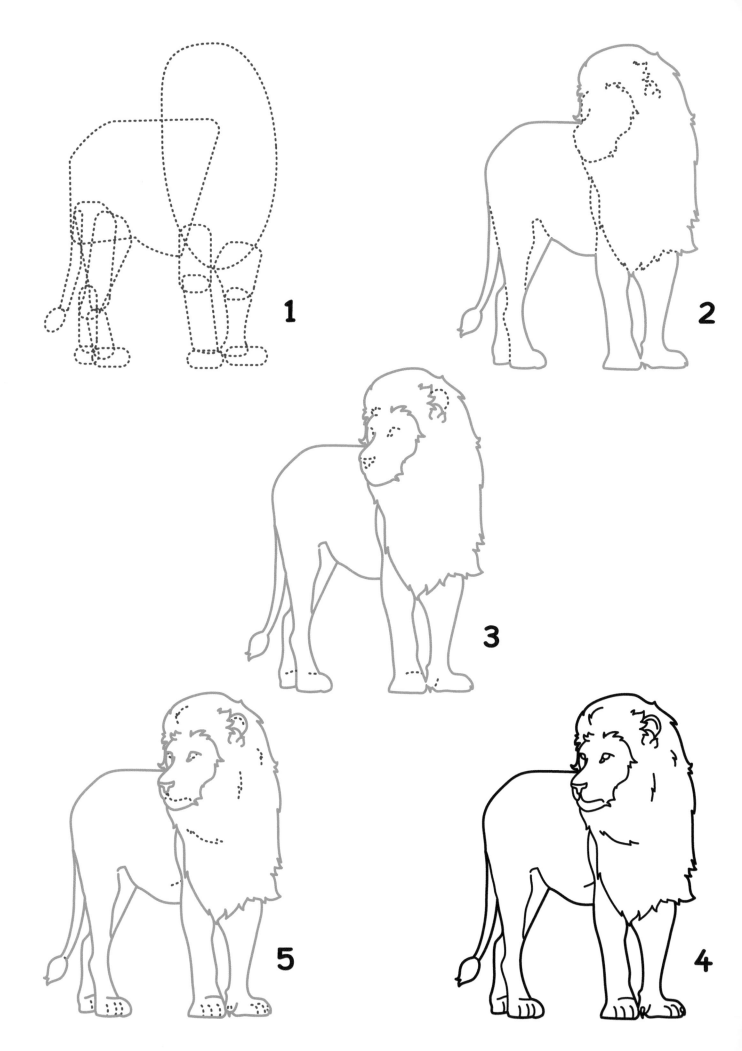

Practice Page

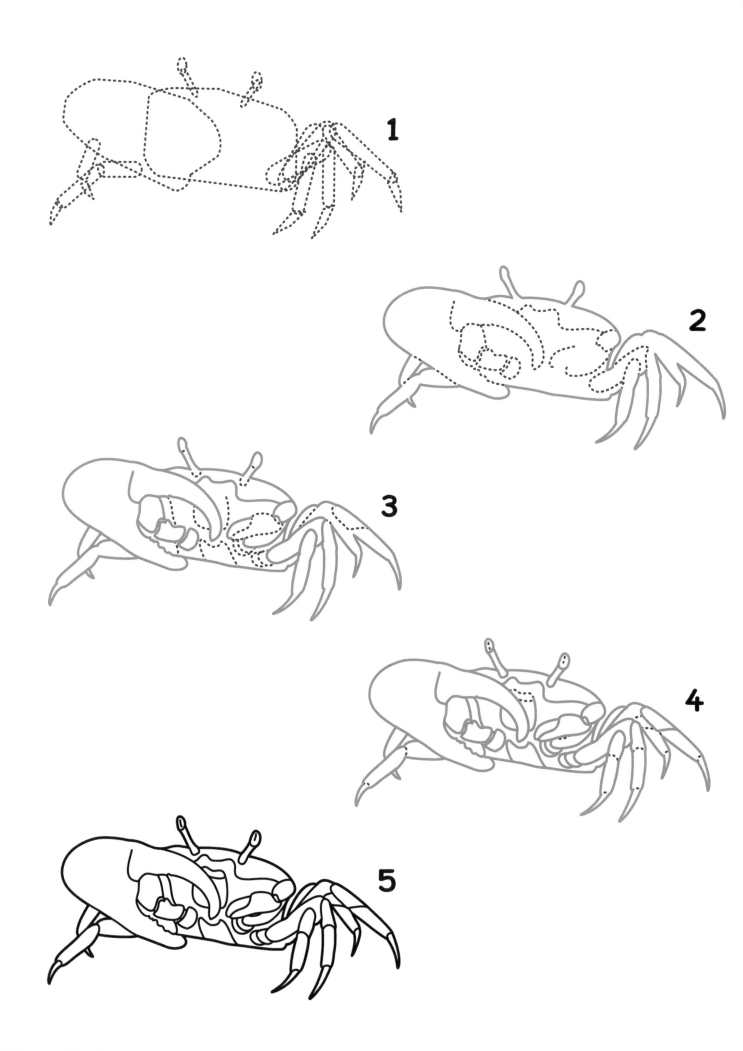

Practice Page

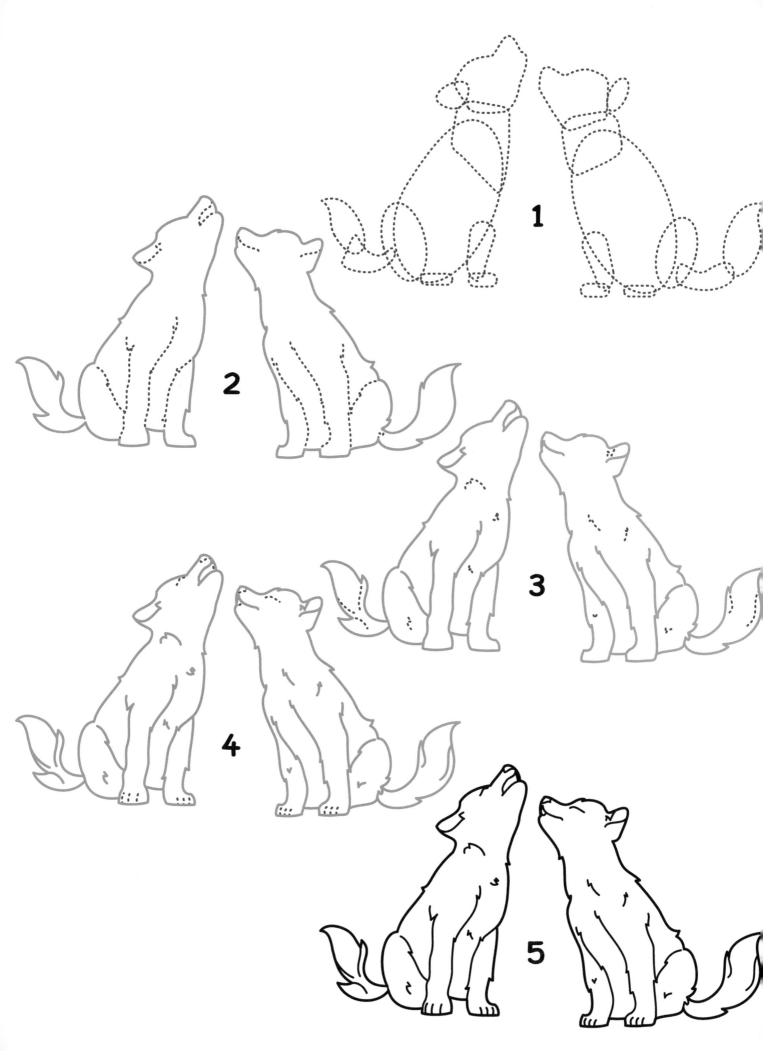

1

2

3

4

5

Practice Page

1

2

3

4

5

Practice Page

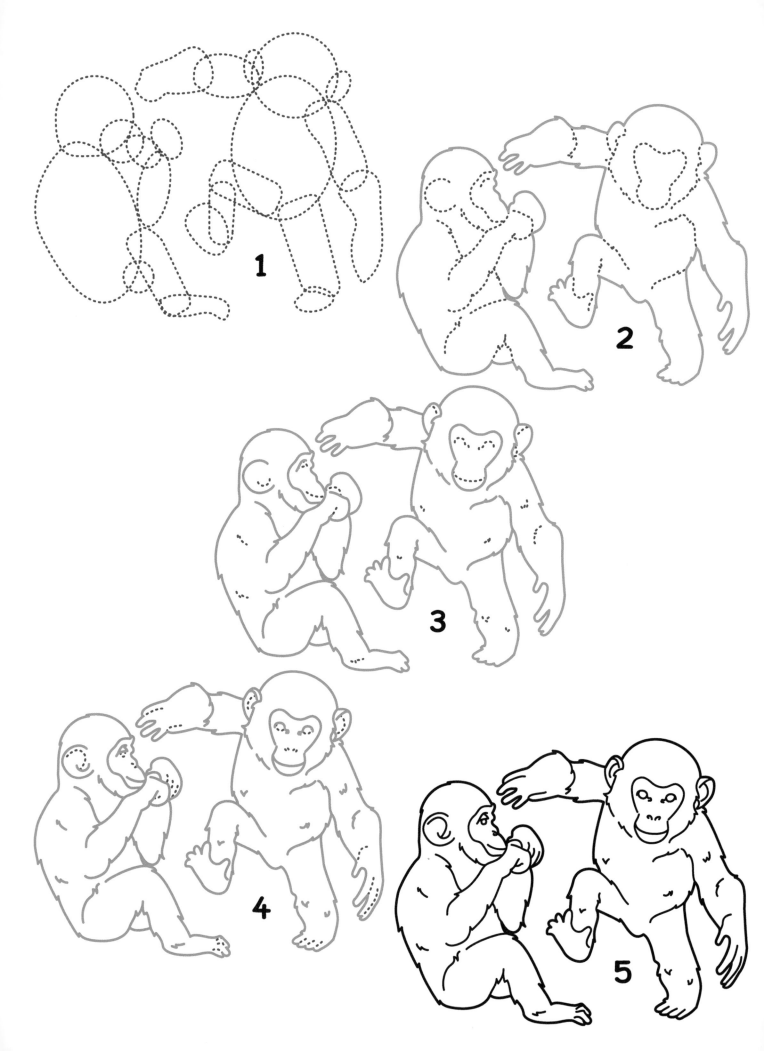

Practice Page

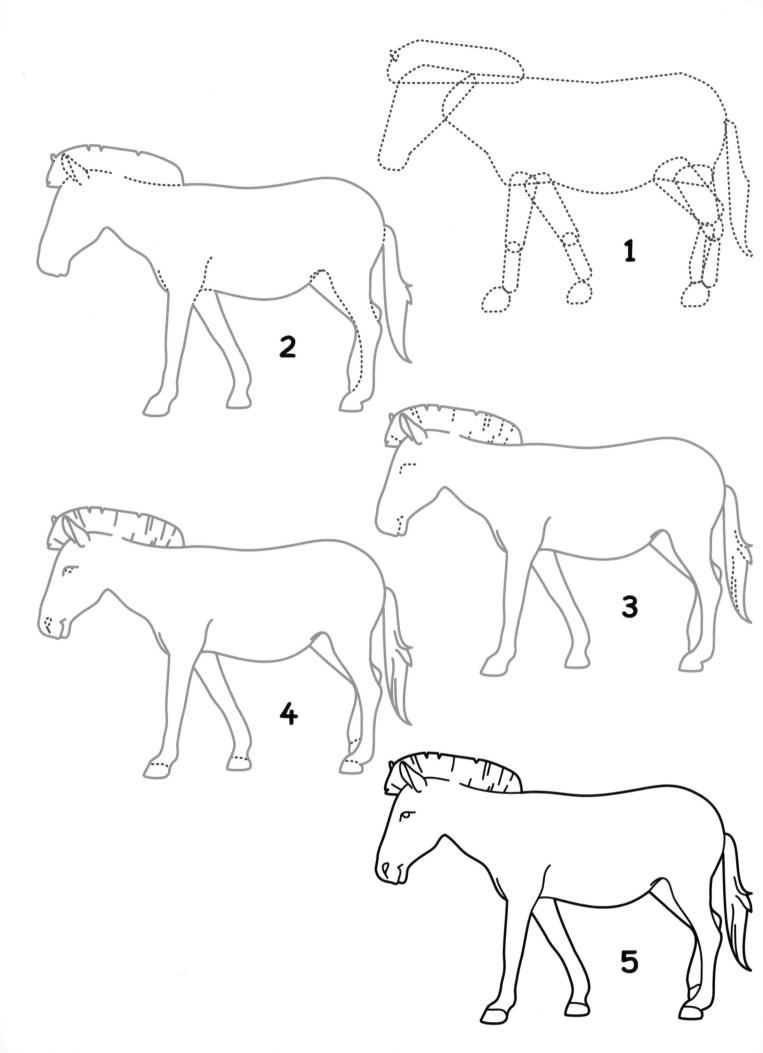

Practice Page

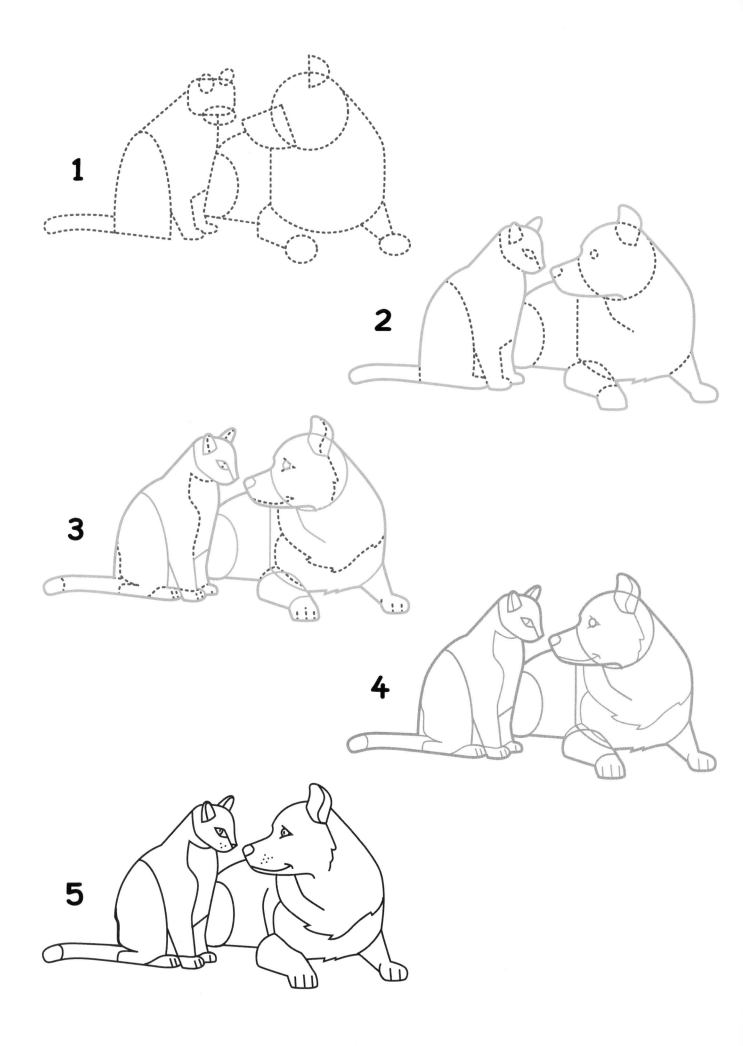

Practice Page

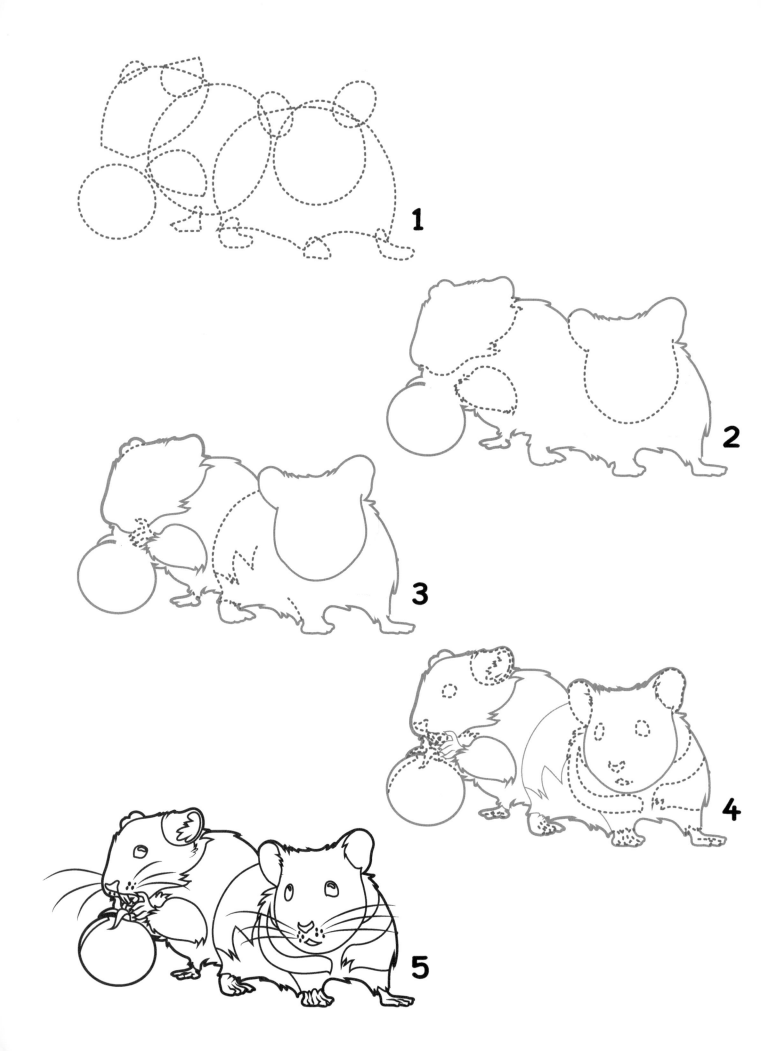

1

2

3

4

5

Practice Page

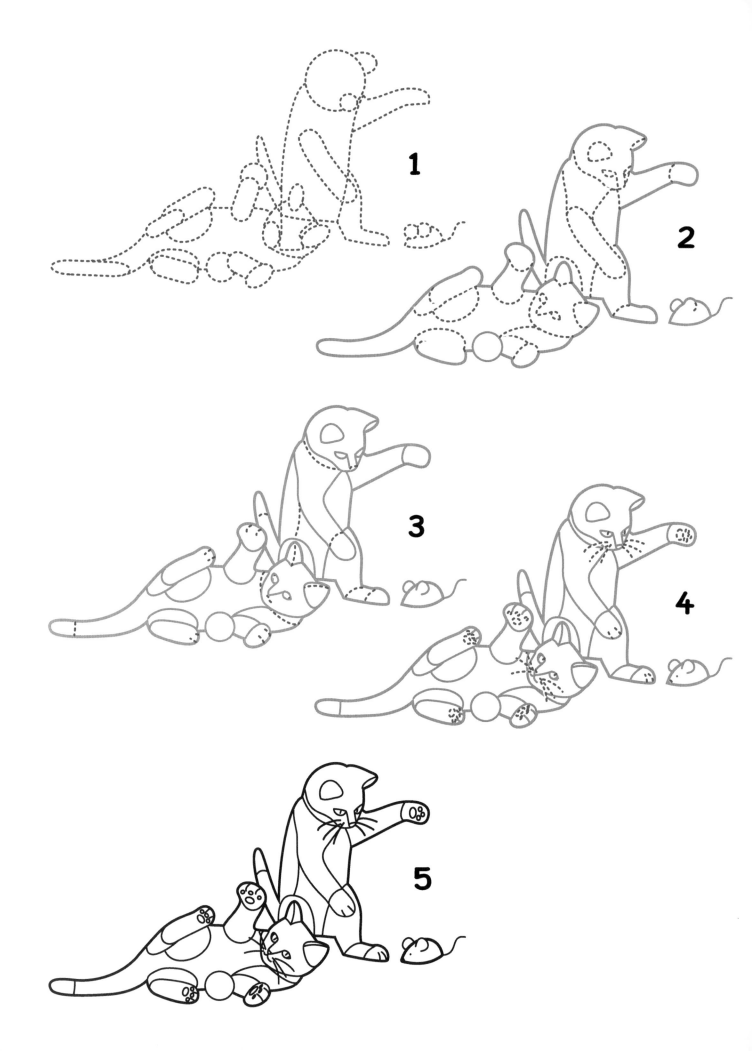

Practice Page

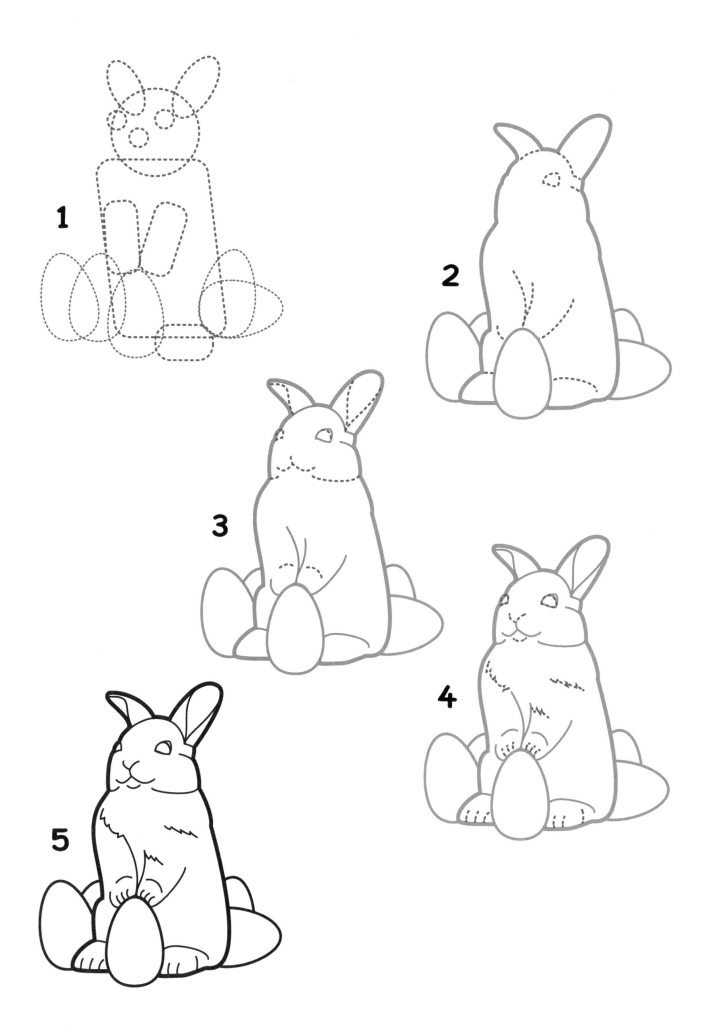

1

2

3

4

5

Practice Page

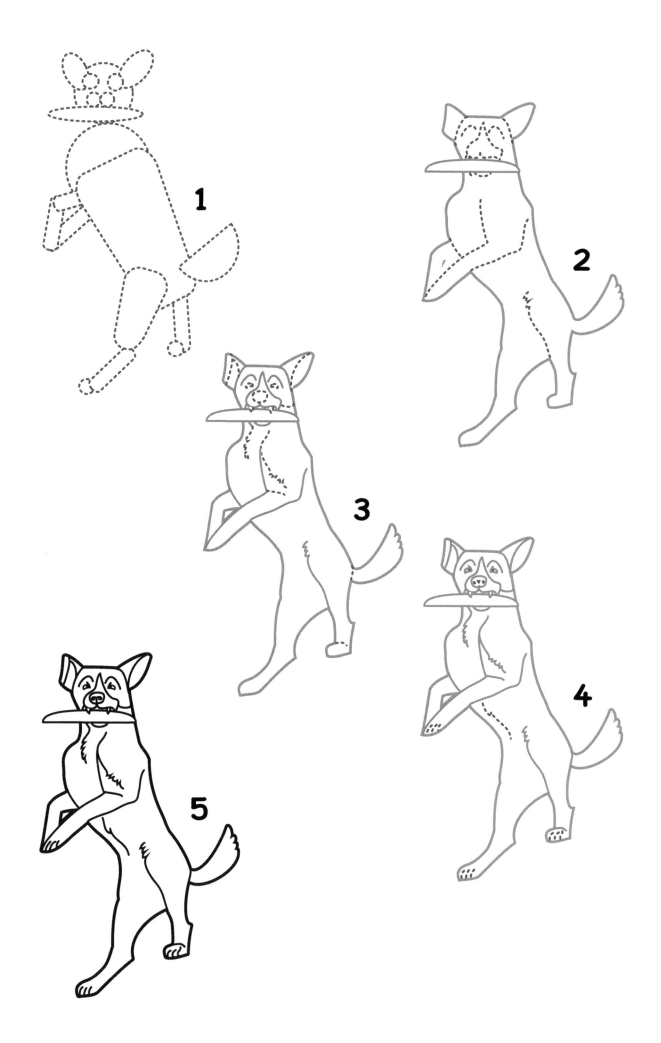

Practice Page

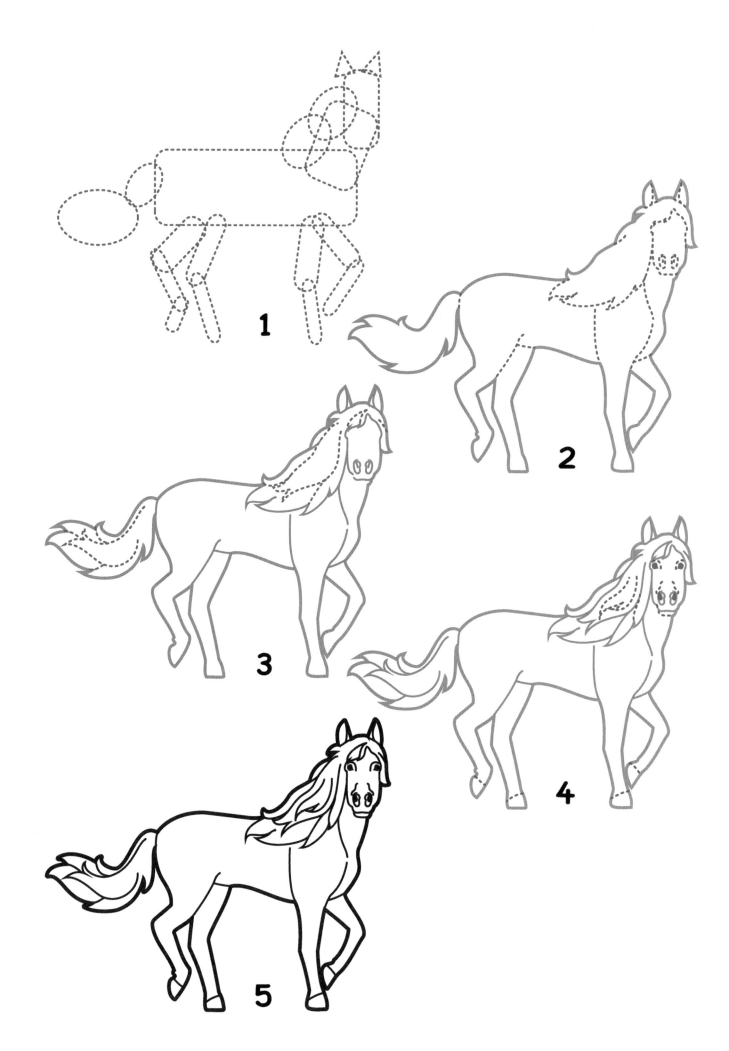

1

2

3

4

5

Practice Page

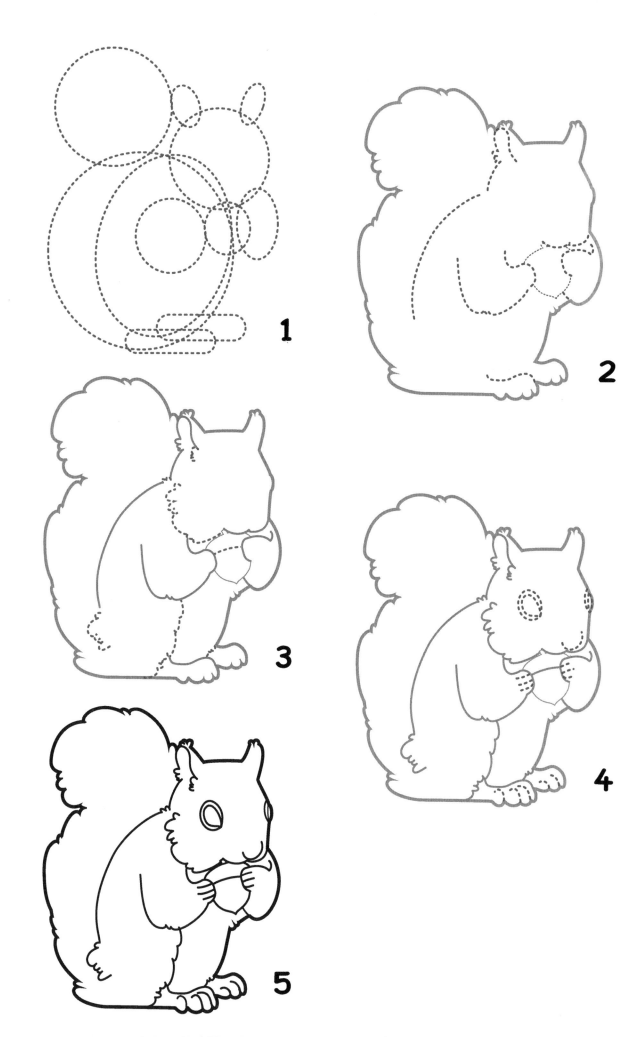

1

2

3

4

5

Practice Page

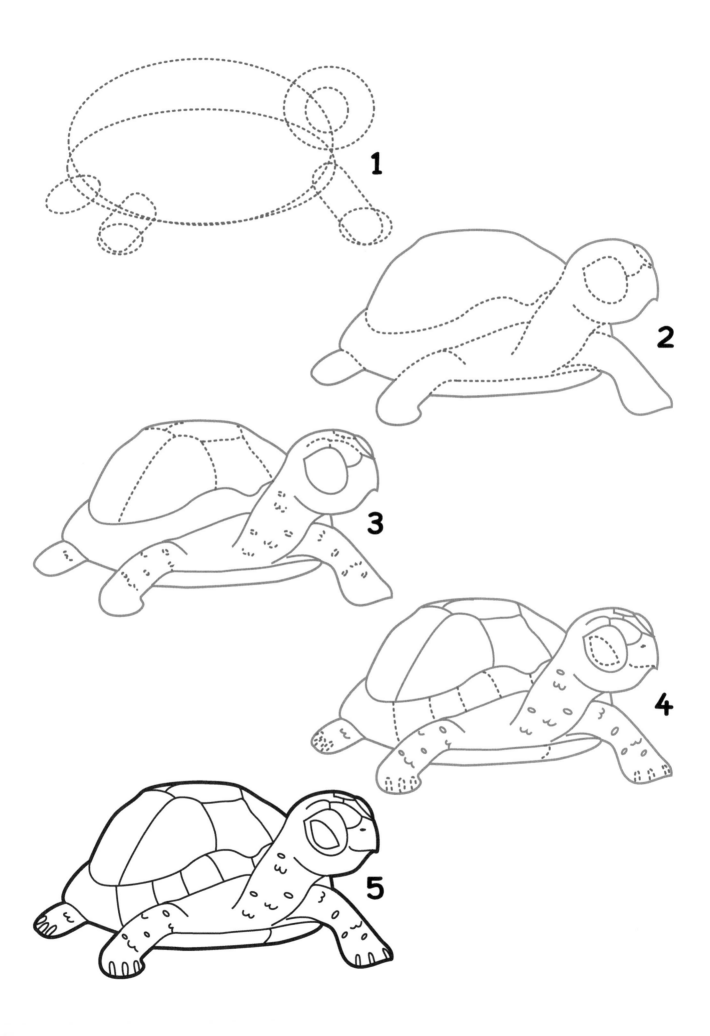

Practice Page

Practice Page

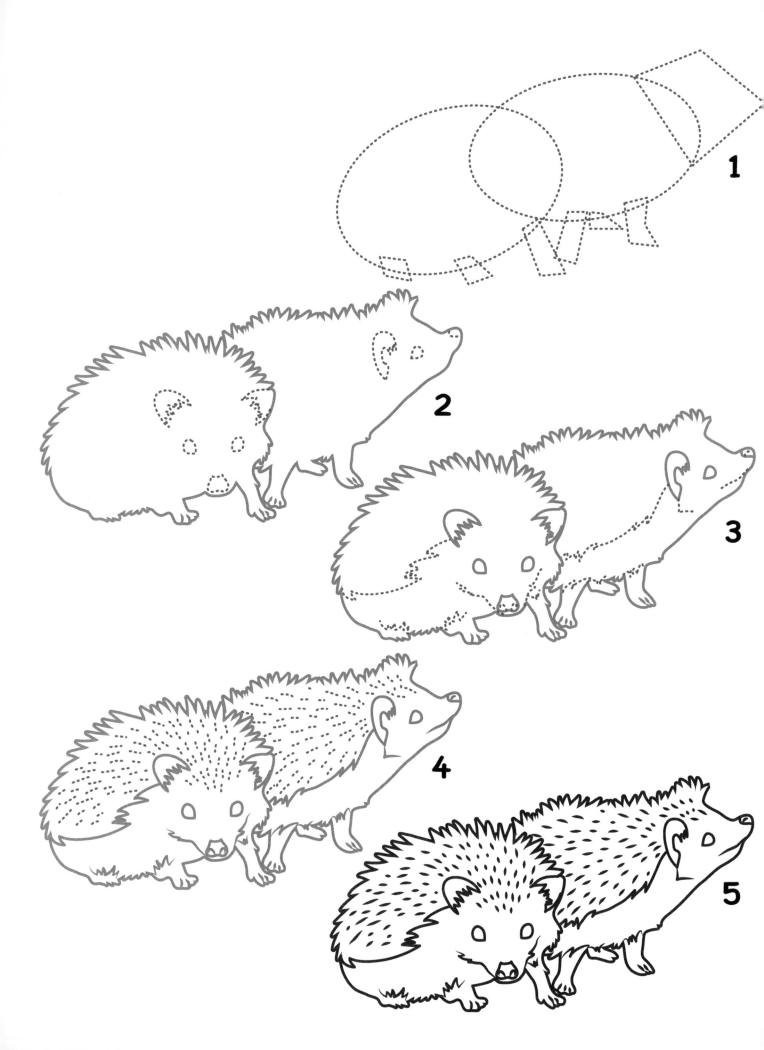

1

2

3

4

5

Practice Page

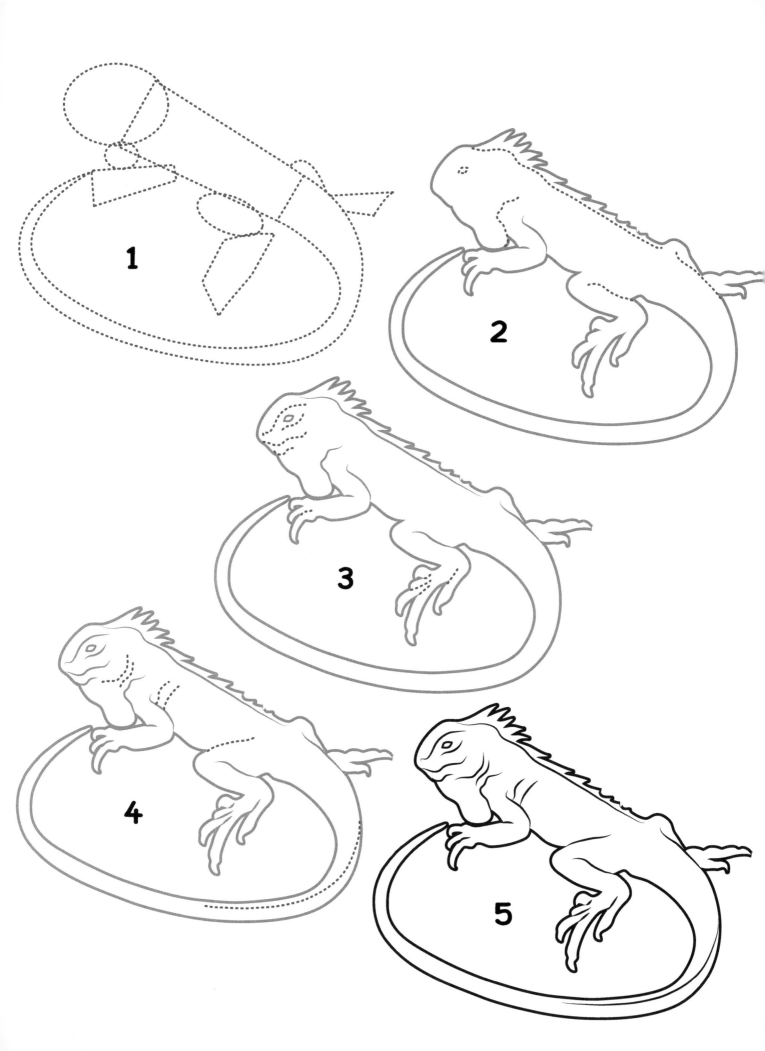

Practice Page

1

2

3

4

5

Practice Page

Practice Page

Practice Page

Practice Page

Practice Page

1

2

3

4

5

Practice Page

Practice Page

Practice Page

1

2

3

4

5

Practice Page

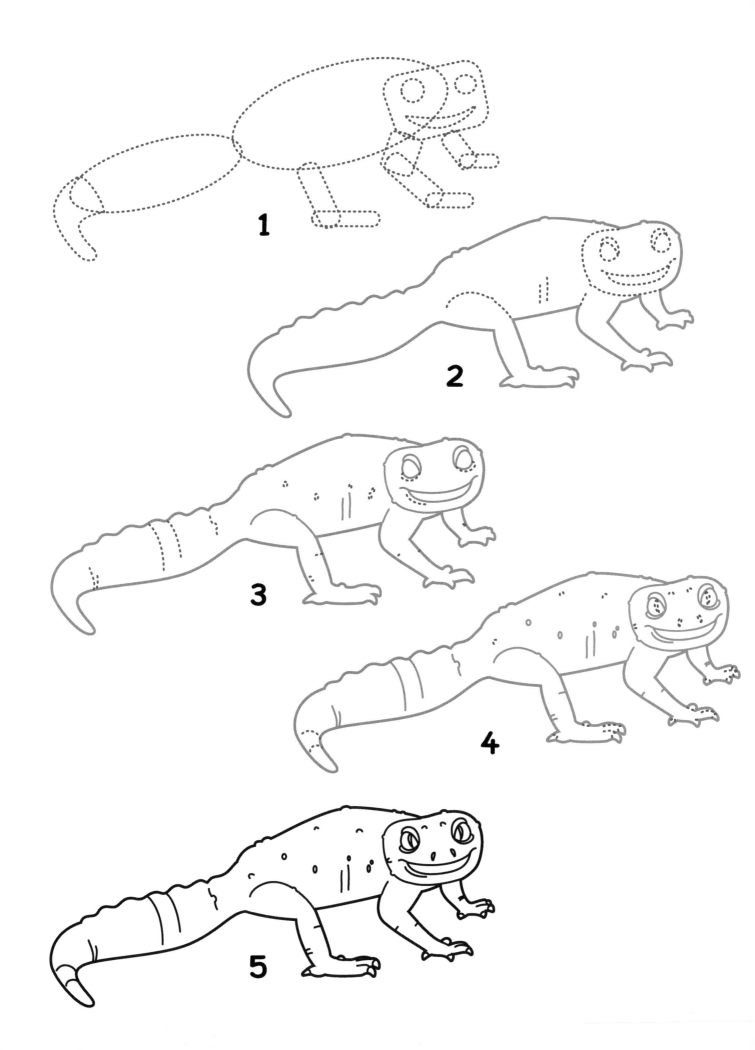

Practice Page

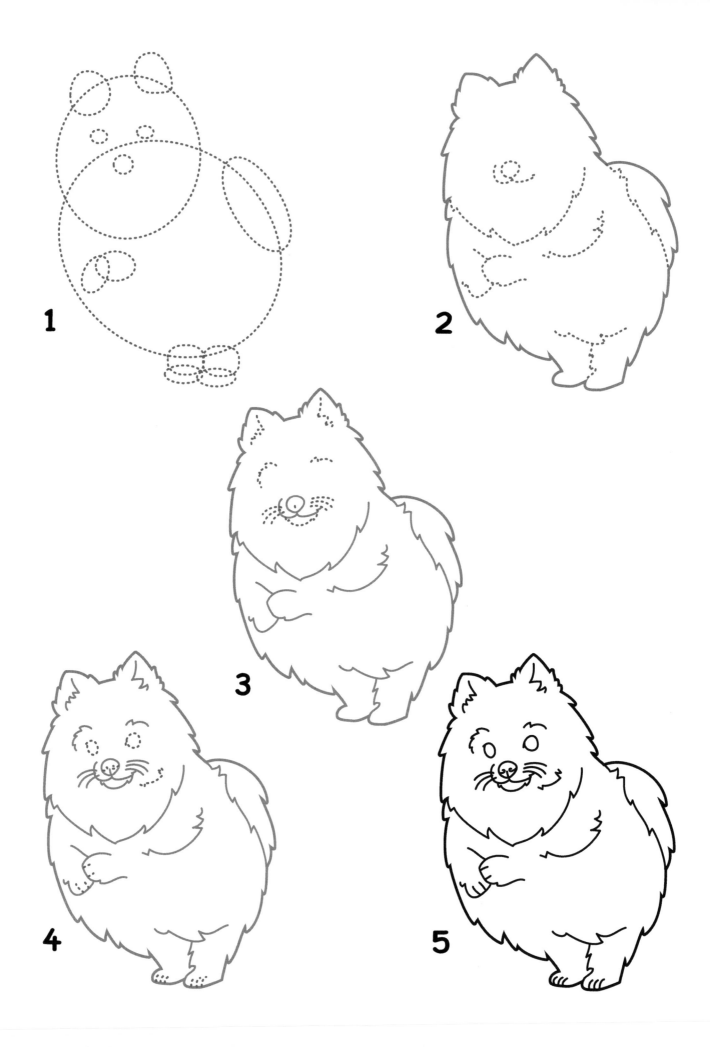

1

2

3

4

5

Practice Page

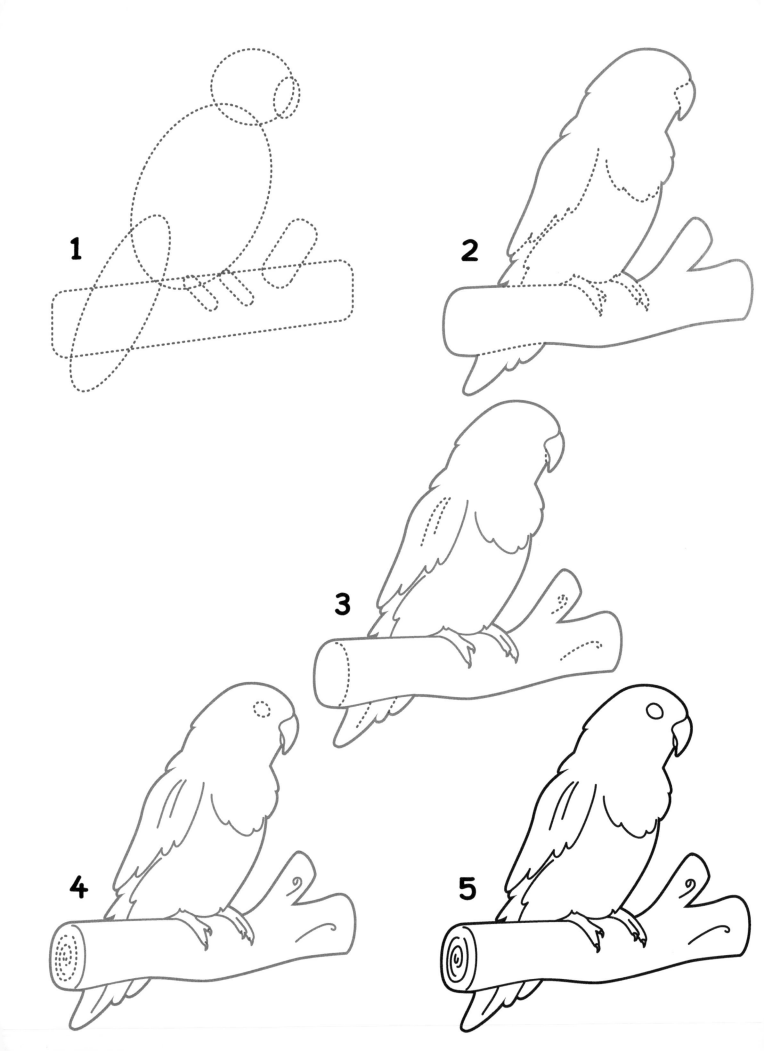

1

2

3

4

5

Practice Page

Practice Page

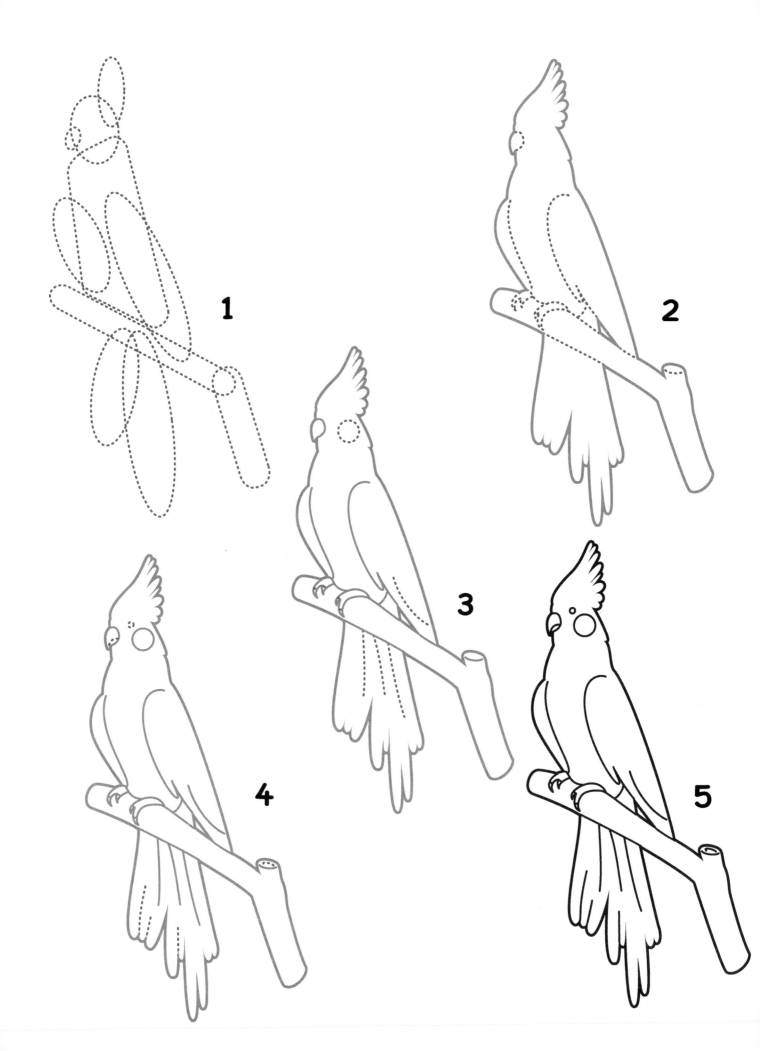

Practice Page

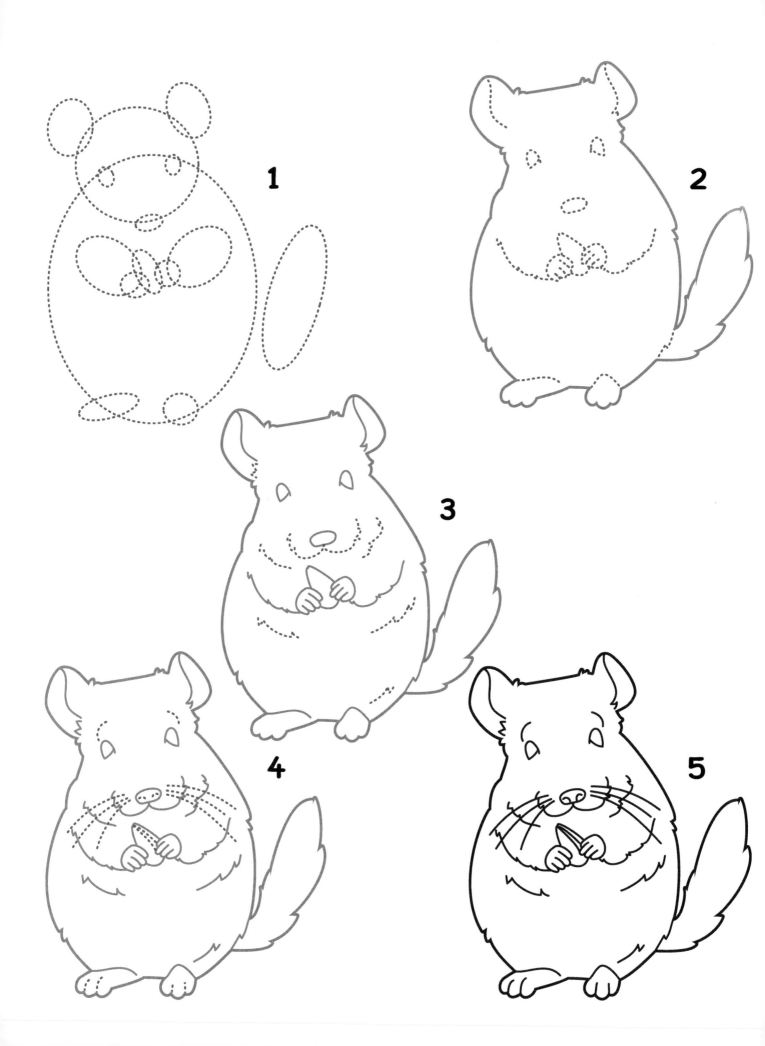

1

2

3

4

5

Practice Page

Practice Page

Practice Page

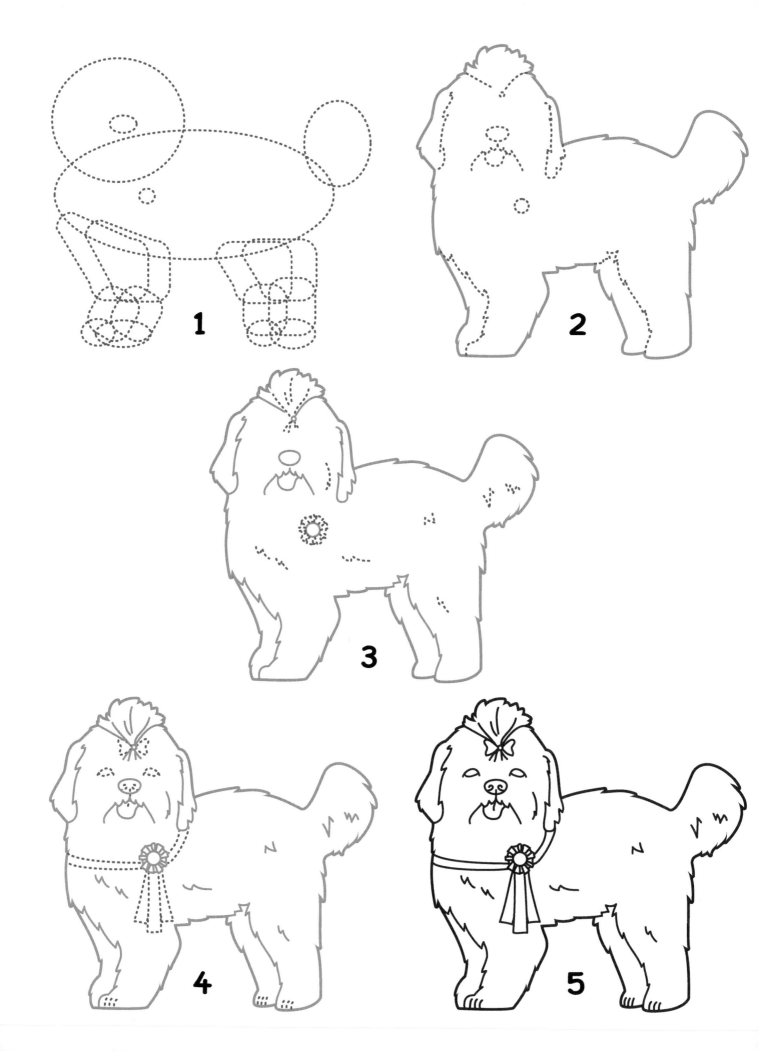

Practice Page

Practice Page

COLORING PAGES

Practice your new skills here!

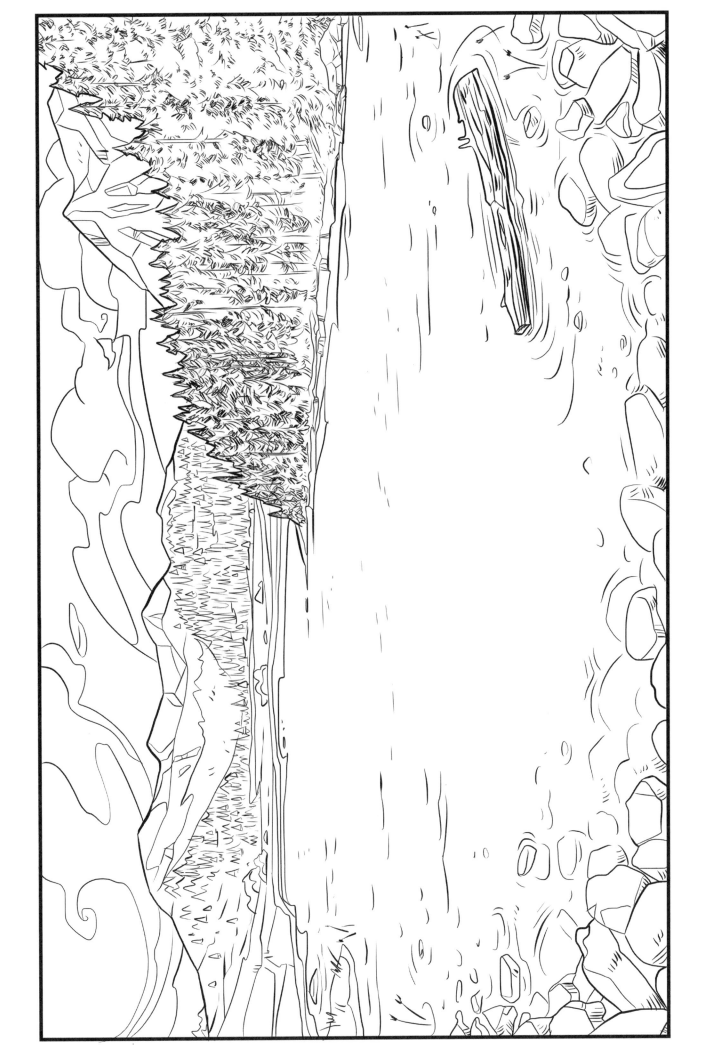

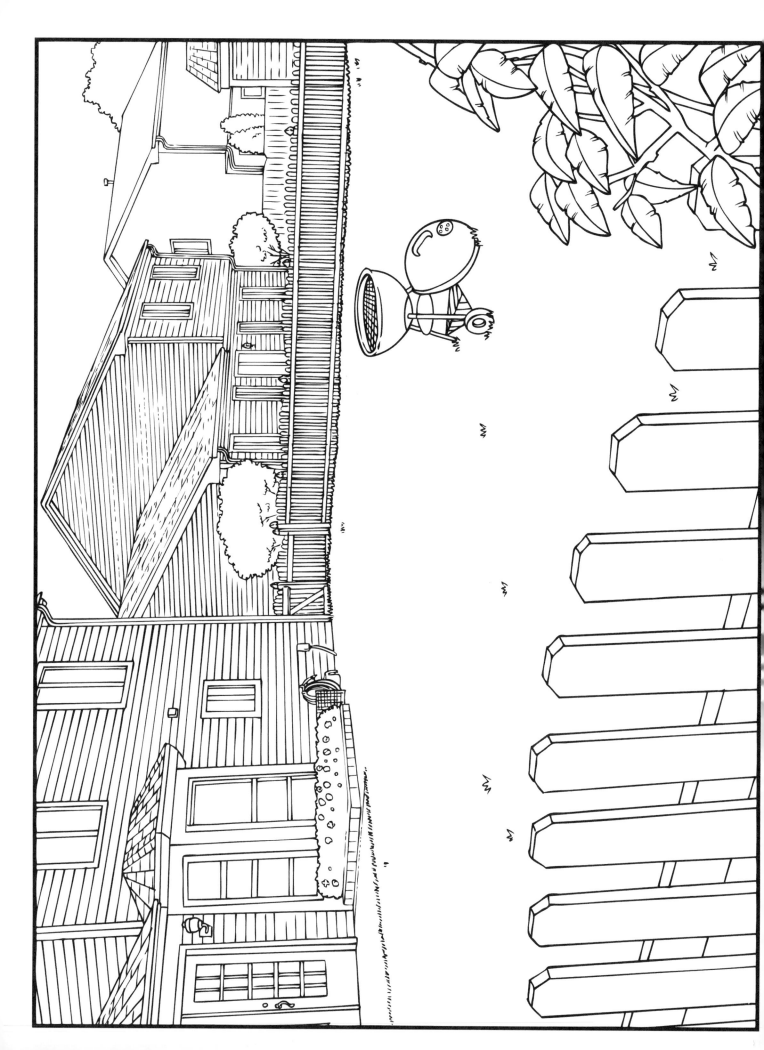

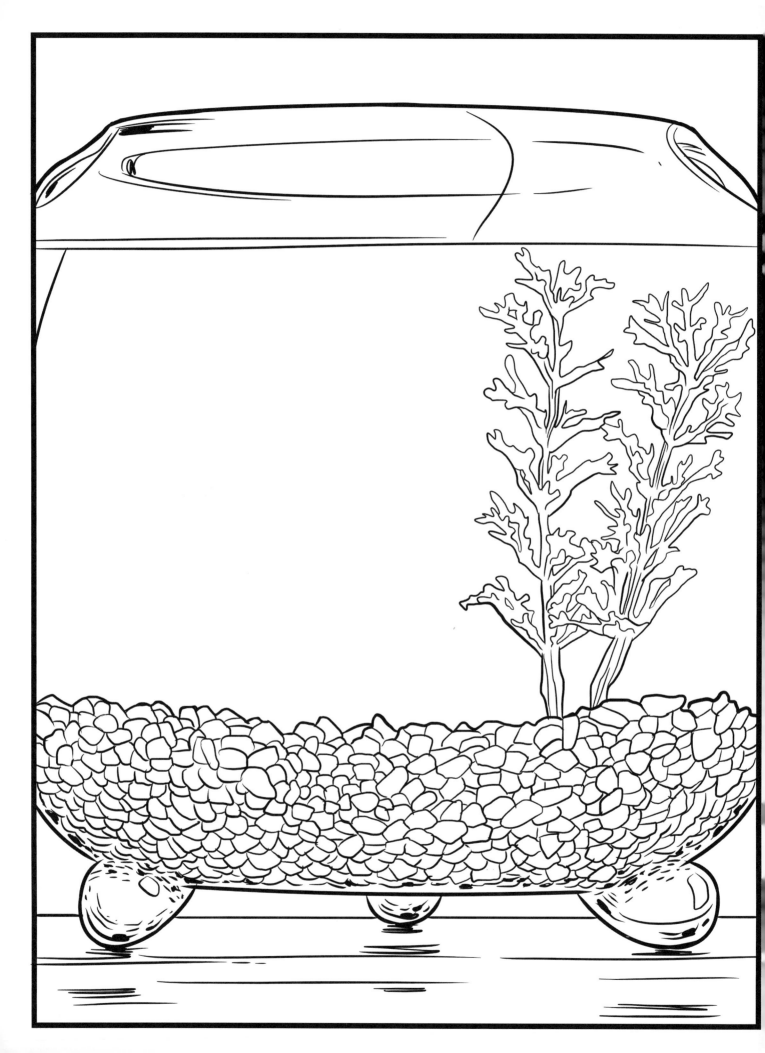

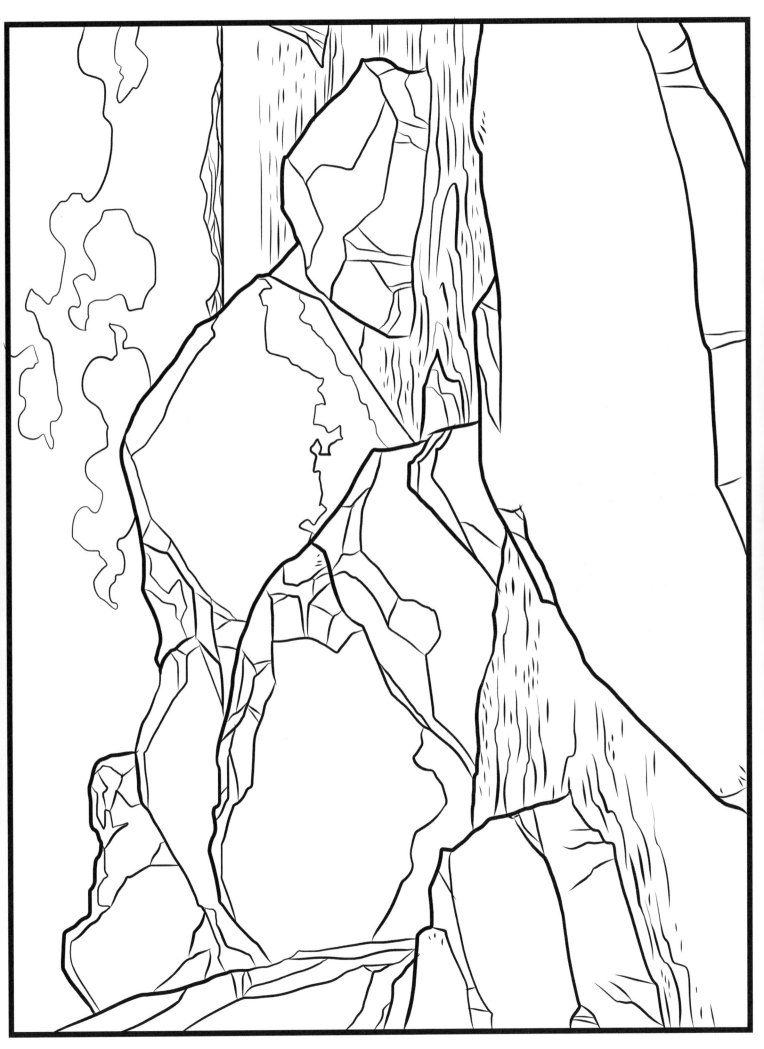